American Girl®

Published by American Girl Publishing

No part of this book may be used or reproduced in any manner whatsoever without written permission except in the case of brief quotations embodied in critical articles and reviews.

19 20 21 22 23 QP 13 12 11 10 9 8 7 6 5 4

Editorial Development: Jennifer Hirsch
Art Direction and Design: Riley Wilkinson and Jessica Annoye
Production: Jeannette Bailey, Kristi Lively, Mary Makarushka, and Cynthia Stiles
Vignettes on pages 96–100 by Flavia Conley

© 2017 American Girl. All American Girl marks are trademarks of American Girl. Marcas registradas utilizadas bajo licencia. American Girl ainsi que les marques et designs y afférents appartiennent à American Girl. **MADE IN CHINA. HECHO EN CHINA. FABRIQUÉ EN CHINE.** Retain this address for future reference: American Girl, 8400 Fairway Place, Middleton, WI 53562, U.S.A. **Importado y distribuido por** A.G. México Retail, S. de R.L. de C.V., Miguel de Cervantes Saavedra No. 193 Pisos 10 y 11, Col. Granada, Delegación Miguel Hidalgo, C.P. 11520 Ciudad de México. Conserver ces informations pour s'y référer en cas de besoin. American Girl Canada, 8400 Fairway Place, Middleton, WI 53562, U.S.A. **Manufactured for and imported into the EU by:** Mattel Europa B.V., Gondel 1, 1186 MJ Amstelveen, Nederland.

For Thu Thai
with thanks

The WellieWishers are a group of fun-loving girls who each have the same big, bright wish: to be a good friend. They love to play in a large and leafy backyard garden cared for by Willa's Aunt Miranda.

Ashlyn

Willa

Emerson

When the WellieWishers step into their colorful garden boots, also known as wellingtons or *wellies*, they are ready for anything—stomping in mud puddles, putting on a show, and helping friendships grow. Like you, they're learning that being kind, creative, and caring isn't always easy, but it's the best way to make friendships bloom.

Camille

Kendall

GARDEN MAP
Carrot's Hutch
Playhouse
Garden Gate
Aunt Miranda's House
Garden Theater Stage

Pond
N
W
E
S
Garden
Shed
Tea Table
Veggie
Garden

Chapter 1

Oodles of Fun

The WellieWishers were very happy. They had finished the last day of school, and the whole summer stretched out ahead of them, full of sunny days.

Yahoo!
Yippee!
Summer! Summer! Summer!
Oh boy!
Hip, hip, hooray!

"Aren't you glad it's summer?" asked Ashlyn.

"Yes! I *love* it! It's *won*derful!" said Emerson.

"Summer days are nice and *looong,*" said Kendall, stretching her hands apart as if she were stretching the word.

"And we can all be in the garden all day *looong,*" added Camille.

"With tons of fun things to do," said Willa.

"Oh, yes, just oodles and *oodles* of fun things to do," said Ashlyn. She tapped her head, saying, "If we use our noodles."

Camille laughed. She balanced the ball on her "noodle" while, to the tune of "Yankee Doodle," she sang:

In the summer
In our garden
If we use our noodles
We'll think up great things to do
And we'll have fun—just oodles!

The WellieWishers giggled at Camille's goofy song.

"Let's put those noodles to work," said Kendall. She got out her notebook and pencil. "Tell me your ideas, and I'll write them down."

"Me first!" said Ashlyn. "You know what would be fun to do on a hot and rainy day? Have a picnic! We'll wear our swimsuits—"

"And wade in mud puddles," added Camille, who loved everything to do with water. "And eat watermelon."

"I think we should put on an acrobat show," said Emerson. "I'll do cartwheels and flips, and maybe a split."

Floop! Emerson spun in a cartwheel.

"Great idea!" said Camille. "Look!

I'll balance the ball on my nose like a sea lion." As she balanced the ball, Camille clapped her arms together as if they were flippers. "Arf, arf, arf," she barked like a sea lion.

"Let's sleep out under the stars some night and count fireflies," said Willa.

"Before we fall asleep, we'll tell stories," said Camille, "about fairies and magic and talking animals."

"Oh, *yes*!" sighed all the girls, happily nodding in agreement.

"Let's build a boat," said Kendall, "and pretend to be explorers."

"Or sailors!" Camille said, saluting. "Aye, aye, sir!"

"We could decorate our boat with rainbows and polka dots and doodles," Kendall continued.

"Doodles?" echoed Camille. She grinned an impish grin. Then once again, to the tune of "Yankee Doodle," Camille sang:

Acrobats and rainy picnics,
Boats with lots of doodles,
Starry skies and fireflies:
We really used our noodles!

Will we have fun? Yes, oodles!
We'll run around like poodles!

Shout,
"Cock-a-
doodle-doodle!"

And eat
some cherry
strudel.

Let's say our
toodle-oodles.

Chapter 2

Come on in, Camille!

The WellieWishers met in the garden early the next morning.

"Which one of our ideas should we try first?" asked Kendall eagerly, looking at the list in her notebook.

"It's very sunny today," sighed Ashlyn. "So I guess we'll just have to wait for a rainy day to have our rainy-day picnic."

“Don’t worry,” said Willa. “It’s bound to rain sometime, and when it does, we’ll have the picnic.”

“I hope I’m here when it rains,” said Camille. “I’d hate to miss the rainy-day picnic.”

"Why would you miss it?" asked Willa.

"My mom signed my sister and me up for ballet every morning. Starting tomorrow, I can only come to the garden in the afternoons," said Camille sadly.

"We'll miss you in the mornings," said Kendall.

"We'll save all the best fun for the afternoon," said Ashlyn.

"Ballet!" gushed Emerson. She rose up on one toe and lifted her arms like a ballerina. "How grown-up. You'll *love* it! It'll be *won*derful! Right?"

"Uh, sure," said Camille. But she didn't sound very sure.

Just then, Aunt Miranda appeared carrying a tray of ice pops. "Help yourselves," she said to the girls.

"Thank you, Aunt Miranda," said the girls as they took the ice pops.

"You're welcome," said Aunt Miranda, waving good-bye as she left.

"Hey," said Willa. She held her ice pop up to her eye as if it were a magnifying glass and looked at the WellieWishers through it. "You all look really *cool. I see* you, *icy* you. Get it?"

"Yes," said Kendall. "I see: we're ice-y."

The girls laughed. But Ashlyn saw that Camille wasn't smiling or laughing.

"What's the matter, Camille?" asked Ashlyn. "Are you feeling sad about missing mornings in the garden with us?"

Camille nodded. "I also miss my grandmother," she said. "She always brings us ice pops, too. But she won't be visiting us this summer."

"Oh, that *is* too bad," said Kendall.

"Before my family moved here last fall, we lived near the ocean, and Granny spent the summer with us," said Camille. "We went to the beach every day."

"You must miss the ocean *and* your grandmother," said Kendall.

"I've never seen the ocean," said Willa. "What's it like?"

"Big," said Camille. "The ocean stretches as far as you can see. And the water changes color all the time. It can look gray or green or blue or silver."

“Oooooh,” sighed the girls.

Emerson said, “It sounds beautiful.”

“It is,” said Camille. “The sand is hot, and the waves are cold and bubbly. They tickle your toes.”

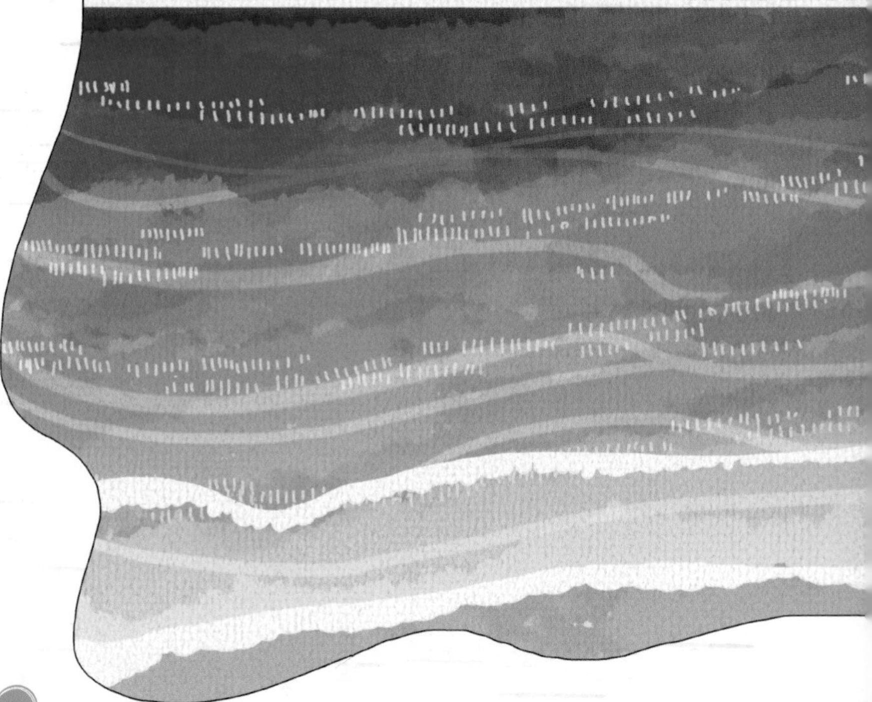

The girls shivered and giggled and wiggled their toes, thinking about the cold, frothy waves.

"The water smells salty and fishy," Camille continued. "Sometimes you see turtles or crabs or seagulls. If you're really lucky, you can see other sea creatures like dolphins and whales swooping up and then diving back into the water—*ker-splash*."

All the girls were quiet, imagining the ocean and the sea creatures Camille described.

"My sister and I used to pretend that we were mermaids," said Camille.

"We'd swim through the water as if our legs were a tail, and sometimes we'd whack the water with our feet, just to make a big splash."

"*Ker-splash!*" said Ashlyn.

"I even made up mermaid stories to tell Granny," said Camille.

"Oh, tell us!" begged Willa.

"I used to imagine that I was a mermaid who lived in an underwater garden full of beautiful shells and wavery sea plants," said Camille.

"The water was bubbly and sunny. The seahorses and dolphins and whales were my friends, and we all played together. Sometimes we'd stick our heads up out of the water and peek at the sailboats and at the people on the shore."

"Ahh," sighed the girls, imagining it.

Emerson said, "Camille, I bet you wish you *were* a mermaid."

Camille nodded. "I do," she said.

"Me, too," said Willa and Ashlyn.

"Dolphin-ately," said Kendall.

Emerson sang to the tune of "Row, Row, Row Your Boat":

Come on in, Camille!
Swim along with me!
Make a wish,
Half girl, half fish,
Splashing in the sea.

Camille said, "One summer, Granny made a mermaid costume for me, but I outgrew it before we moved. Now my sister says I'm too big to play mermaid anyway."

"What?" said Emerson. "No one is *ever* too big to play mermaid."

"Dolphin-ately *not*," agreed Kendall.

"Probably your sister was just being *crabby*," said Willa.

"She didn't say it to upset you on *porpoise*," said Ashlyn.

Camille knew that her friends were trying to cheer her up with their silly puns. "It's okay," she said. "I couldn't play mermaid anymore even if I *did* have a mermaid tail. Mermaids can't live on dry land, and the ocean can't fit in Aunt Miranda's garden."

When Camille left to go home, Ashlyn said, “Camille sounded sad. Let’s try to help her feel better. What can we do?”

The girls thought for a moment. Suddenly, Willa looked up, grinning. “Guess what?” she said, “I have a *whale* of a plan!”

Chapter 3

Something Fishy

The next morning, Aunt Miranda came to the shed to get a wheelbarrow.

"Whoa!" she exclaimed when she saw the girls at work. "What on earth are you girls doing?"

Kendall was wet and covered with bubbles.

Ashlyn was polka-dotted with paint.

Emerson was sitting in the middle of a sea of paper scraps.

Willa said, "It's a secret."

"Camille is sad that she can't come to the garden in the mornings," said Emerson, "so we're making a surprise for her. Promise you won't tell?"

"I promise," said Aunt Miranda. She grinned. "I wouldn't know what to say anyway, because I can't tell what you're making here, except a wonderful mess. What is this?"

"It's going to be an underwater garden," Willa said, "because Camille wants to be a mermaid."

"Her granny made her a mermaid's tail, but she outgrew it," said Ashlyn.

"Camille can't go to the ocean," explained Kendall. "So we're bringing the ocean to her."

Ashlyn swiped her forehead with the back of her hand. "It's harder than we thought it was going to be," she admitted. "But it'll be worth it if it makes Camille happy."

"We'll *all* be happy when it's finished," said Willa.

"You mean when it's *fin*-ished," joked Kendall. She put the palms of her hands together and turned them left and right, like a fish's fins. "I hope we can keep it a secret until then."

"Don't worry," said Aunt Miranda. "I'll keep your secret." She winked. "It'll be easy: I'll just *clam* up."

But keeping the underwater garden a secret from Camille was not easy for the girls.

The very next afternoon, they were at the old shed working hard on their underwater garden. Willa was putting stuffing into a pillow, and Ashlyn was painting pink flowers on the tub. Emerson was making paper cutouts of sea creatures, and Kendall was fiddling with the water faucet.

Suddenly, they heard Camille call from just inside the gate. “Yoo-hoo! Hello! I’m here! Where is everybody?”

"Eeek!" squeaked Willa. "Camille is here already, and I'm covered with pillow fluff! Quick, Ashlyn, meet her at the gate and stall her. We can't let her see what we're doing. Give us time to hide this stuff in the shed."

"I can't go!" whispered Ashlyn. "Camille will ask why I'm all spattered with pink paint."

"Tell her it's not paint," said Emerson, who was frantically gathering up scraps of paper scattered all over the ground. "Tell her—tell her that you've got a poison ivy rash."

"That won't work," Ashlyn wailed. "Camille can tell this pink paint isn't poison ivy."

"I'll go," said Kendall.

"Hurry up!" whispered Willa.

Kendall wiped her wet hands on her skirt as she hurried to meet Camille. "Hi, Camille," she said nervously.

"How come you're all wet?" asked Camille.

"Oh, I was just fiddling around with the faucet," said Kendall. She changed the subject before Camille could ask *why*. "So how was ballet this morning?"

"Fine," answered Camille. "We learned the plié." She started to walk toward the playhouse, but Kendall held her back.

"What's a plié?" asked Kendall.

"It's sort of a squat," said Camille.

"Oh, please show me!" said Kendall.

"Well, okay," said Camille. "It's like this." She turned her toes out, bent her knees, sank down, and rose up again.

"Like this?" asked Kendall, copying Camille.

"Yup, good," said Camille, starting again toward the playhouse. "Come on, let's—"

"Wait!" said Kendall, desperately trying to give the other girls more time. "That looks fun." She sank down and bounced up in a plié, then did it again, saying, "I like it!"

Kendall was relieved when the other girls came running up to the gate. They all looked a little red in the face. "What are you two doing?" asked Emerson, out of breath.

"Camille learned pliés this morning," said Kendall. "Look!" She sank down and bounced up to show the other girls.

"Pliés!" cheered the girls, sinking down and bouncing up like boing-y kangaroos.

Camille asked her friends, "What did *you* do this morning?"

"Oh, you know, just stuff," answered Willa casually.

Camille pointed to some paint on Ashlyn's hand. "Are you painting?" she asked.

"Painting?" repeated Ashlyn, looking at her dotty hand. "Well, um, I guess so. I mean, kind of."

Camille looked confused.

Quickly, Emerson said, "We were mostly just waiting for you. So now that you're here, let's do something fun."

"Let's do one of our plans!" said Kendall, waving her notebook. "Remember?" She sang to the tune of "Yankee Doodle":

Acrobats and rainy picnics,
Boats with lots of doodles,
Starry skies and fireflies:
We really used our noodles!

"There's an old tin tub in the gardening shed," said Camille. "We could pretend it's a boat. Come on!"

She headed toward the shed. "Let's go find it. We can clean it up, and paint it, and—"

"No!" said the other girls all at once. They blocked Camille's way to the shed.

Camille stopped short, puzzled. She began, "Why don't you want—?"

Kendall talked over her. "Let's not do that boat plan right now," she said briskly. "Let's plan our acrobat show instead!"

"Hooray!" said Emerson. "A show!"

Camille was surprised, and a bit hurt at being snubbed and ignored. But no one seemed to notice, because they were all swept away by Emerson, who commanded, "Everyone come with me!"

Emerson ran to the stage, leading the girls. "So! Who has an idea?" she asked.

No one said anything.

"Don't *you* have any ideas, Emerson?" asked Camille. "You usually have millions."

"Sure!" said Emerson. "Let's see. I know! I'll do my cartwheel, and you can balance the ball, and then, uh, and then . . ." she petered out.

Willa piped up, "I've got a great idea for a solo act."

"But you hate solos," said Camille.

Willa ignored her. She climbed up onto the stage. "I'll do pliés and sing new words I've made up to 'Row, Row, Row Your Boat,'" she said. "Listen." Willa held out the edges of her skirt. As she sank down and rose up awkwardly, she sang:

Down, up, down and up,
Bend your knees and squat,
Something, something,
something, something.
Doing some pliés.

"I *love* it," gushed Emerson. "It's *won*derful." Ashlyn and Kendall said nothing, but clapped politely.

“Shouldn’t your song rhyme?” asked Camille.

“Don’t worry, I’ll figure that out later,” said Willa, brushing off Camille’s question as if it were a pesky fly.

"Ohhh-kay," said Camille. She was surprised that Emerson, who loved to write songs, wasn't suggesting improvements to Willa's. And since when did Willa want to be alone on the stage singing and dancing all by herself? When the WellieWishers had put on their fall show, Willa had refused to do a solo.

Camille thought her friends were not behaving like themselves at all!

Chapter 4

Half In, Half Out

Argh!" wailed Willa the next morning. "I can't stand it. I hate hiding the truth from Camille. Can't we tell her when she comes today?"

"And ruin the surprise?" asked Emerson.

"The surprise is ruining our *friendship,*" said Ashlyn. "We hurt Camille's feelings yesterday when we shouted 'No!' about the boat. I think we should tell her what we're doing."

"The underwater garden is *almost* done," said Kendall. "She'll find out soon."

"We've kept quiet *this* long," said Emerson. "Let's not give up now. We'll just have to work harder and finish faster."

"Let's give Camille the surprise as soon as we can," said Willa. "I can tell that she thinks we're acting weird."

"That's for sure," Kendall nodded. "Camille knows something fishy is going on."

Kendall was right. Camille *did* think something fishy was going on. That afternoon as she walked to the garden after ballet, she thought about how odd and jumpy her friends had acted the day before. They had ignored her suggestions, and when she had asked them questions, their answers were slippery. Camille was pretty sure that the other WellieWishers were hiding something from her, which made her feel left out and lonely and sad.

Just outside the garden gate, Camille saw Aunt Miranda weeding.

"I'm glad to see you, Camille," said Aunt Miranda. "I haven't seen you as often as usual lately."

"That's because I'm only here in the afternoons," said Camille. She sighed. "Sometimes I think maybe it would be better if I just didn't come to the garden at all."

Aunt Miranda sat back on her heels. "Why's that?" she asked.

"Because being half in and half out is hard," said Camille. "I like ballet, but I miss being with the

WellieWishers. I feel left out, as if I don't know what they're doing." She paused, then went on, "I love summer in the garden, but I miss being with my grandmother at the ocean. I feel as if no matter where I am, I'm not where I want to be."

"I know what you mean," said Aunt Miranda. "I love to travel, but I miss the garden when I'm away. So I close my eyes and imagine it. That always makes me feel better."

That evening at home, Camille thought about what Aunt Miranda had said. She closed her eyes and took a deep breath. Suddenly, she could imagine the ocean so well that she could almost smell it—all salty and tangy and fishy—and feel the water's spray tickling her skin.

Camille didn't want to lose the picture she had in her mind, so she began to draw it. And when it was done, she wrote down one of the mermaid stories that she used to tell her grandmother.

After writing, Camille felt as if a big, heavy weight had been lifted from her heart. The sadness of missing Granny and the ocean and the hurt of being left out by her friends were lessened. She felt light and free, the way she did when she was in the ocean and a huge wave tossed her up, up, up like a flying fish.

Drawing and writing about the ocean made Camille feel so much better that she decided to draw more pictures and write down all the mermaid stories she could remember and put them together in a book.

Chapter 5

Tales and Tails

A few days later, when Camille stepped inside the garden gate, she was surprised. Inside her wellington boot was a bottle. And inside the bottle was a message:

Come to the old shed.

"How mysterious," thought Camille. She ran as fast as she could to the shed. And when she got there . . .

"Surprise!" shouted all the WellieWishers.

"Oh, oh, *oh*," breathed Camille. "This is *beautiful*!"

"It's your underwater garden," said

Kendall excitedly. "The one from the mermaid story that you told us."

"We loved your mermaid story so much that we wanted to make it come true for you," said Willa.

“And we were so sorry that you couldn’t visit the ocean this summer, we tried to bring the ocean to you,” said Ashlyn.

Emerson was too bouncy to speak. She burst out singing to the tune of “Row, Row, Row Your Boat”:

Come on in, Camille!
Swim along with me!
Make a wish,
Half girl, half fish
Splashing in the sea.

Camille knelt on the sand and dipped her hand into the tub. “The sand is hot, and the water is cold,” she said. "And these bubbles tickle me just like the ocean spray." She held the seashell to her ear. "I can hear the ocean in this shell." She beamed at her friends and said, "I really feel as if I'm at the ocean."

"Here's your seahorse friend," said Willa. She swam a pillow shaped like a seahorse into Camille's arms.

"And some pretty sunglasses," said Emerson as she put them on Camille.

"You can keep time with the sand in your hourglass," said Kendall, as she flipped it over.

"And put treasures in your treasure chest," said Ashlyn as she held it up.

Camille smiled. "Now I see what you were doing while I was not here: You were making lots and lots of surprises for me!" she said. "Thank you!"

And her friends replied,

Camille lifted the lid of the treasure chest and took out a package wrapped in brown paper.

"Hey," said Willa, "what's that?"

"Isn't it another present from all of you?" asked Camille.

"No," said her friends.

"Open it, open it, open it," said Emerson, practically bursting with curiosity.

When Camille opened the package, the other WellieWishers were as surprised as she was. Because inside the package there was . . .

"A mermaid tail," sighed all the WellieWishers blissfully.

"I *love* it," said Emerson. "It's *won*derful!"

"There's a crown, too," said Ashlyn.

"I'll help you put it on, Camille," said Willa.

Camille spun so that her mermaid tail sparkled and glistened in the sunshine, as if it were wet with ocean spray. "It fits perfectly!" said Camille happily.

"Where did it come from?" asked Ashlyn.

"Here's a note," said Kendall.

Dear Camille,

Your friend Aunt Miranda called me. She told me that you missed your mermaid tail, so I made you a new one. I hope you are never too big to imagine you're a mermaid.

Love and kisses ♡

Granny ☺

For a moment, Camille couldn't say anything. She was so overwhelmed with gratitude that she had a lump in her throat and tears pricked her eyes. She was thankful—and she was pleased, too, because it was her description of the ocean and her mermaid story that had given her friends the inspiration for the underwater garden.

Suddenly, Camille thought of a way to thank her friends.

Camille took her book of mermaid stories out of her backpack. "I wrote down some of my mermaid tales," she told the other WellieWishers. Then she grinned. "While Granny was making a mermaid *tail*, I was making mermaid *tales*. Look!"

Mermaid
Tales

"Oooooh," breathed the girls as they crowded close to look at Camille's book of mermaid tales.

The mermaid swam next to a boat. The boat had rainbows, polka dots, and doodles on it.
Splish, splash in the sea.
Hello friendly whale!
Come along and swim with me in my mermaid's tale.

"Isn't this the best book you've ever read?" asked Willa.

"Dolphin-ately!" said Kendall.

Emerson said, "I *love* it. It's *won*derful."

"This is o-*fish*-ally my favorite book ever," said Ashlyn.

Camille hugged Granny's note to her chest. As she watched her friends looking at her book, she felt very happy and peaceful, as if she and Granny and her wonderful WellieWisher friends were all together beside the beautiful sea.

For Parents

The Power of Storytelling

Children are natural storytellers. Stories are more than just entertainment: They can help us remember good times, work through worries, and even satisfy wishes. When Camille missed the fun she used have playing mermaid by the ocean, she wrote a story about it, which made her feel better. Imagination is also a stepping-stone to success: Just as athletes imagine winning a competition, children can imagine themselves overcoming problems and achieving their goals. Use the power of storytelling and imagination to help your little girl deal with something in her life that she wishes were different.

- **If she's missing someone**—such as an absent parent, grandparent, or friend—help her stay connected by telling a story in which she joins that person on an adventure. Offer simple

prompts, such as, "One day, Grandma heard the doorbell ring. She opened her door, and *you* were standing there! What did you say to Grandma? . . . And then what happened?" Write down her story, and have her add a few illustrations. Then make a copy and send it to the person in the story!

- **If she has trouble with something,** like waiting patiently, ask her, "What if there was a contest to see who could wait the longest? What would the prize be? What if some of the kids just couldn't wait—what would happen?" Then talk about the possibilities. If they are silly, so much the better—humor is a great way to defuse frustration.

- **If your girl has a heartfelt wish** that isn't easily fulfilled, help her imagine it coming true. For example, together you could make up a story about a girl (with her name, of course) who has a pony. Add details, such as where the pony lives and what the neighbors say when they see her riding down the street. If you live in a city, here's your chance to face some of the problems of having a horse in a humorous way. Maybe the pony has to live in the bathroom and eat hay out of the bathtub!

Make a real book

To share your young author's work with others or to preserve it, scan her writings and art into a computer. Then, using a photo website or copy shop, have her work bound into a real book. Consider giving copies as gifts to important people in her life. Or you can make a book the old-fashioned way by lining up the pages, punching holes along the left side, and sewing the pages together with a ribbon. Don't forget to have her create a cover with her name on it as the author and illustrator!

Art from the heart

Sometimes it's easier to tell a story in pictures. Help your young artist create a collage inside a heart to show what she loves. Cut out a large heart from poster board or paper, and have her draw or glue pictures on it of things she loves—people, pets, and favorite places—using markers, family photos, and pictures from magazines. Just thinking about what to include in her collage will make her heart happy.

About the Author

VALERIE TRIPP says that she became a writer because of the kind of person she is. She says she's curious, and writing requires you to be interested in everything. Talking is her favorite sport, and writing is a way of talking on paper. She's a daydreamer, which helps her come up with her ideas. And she loves words. She even loves the struggle to come up with just the right words as she writes and rewrites. Ms. Tripp lives in Maryland with her husband.

Parents, request a FREE catalog at **americangirl.com/catalog.**
Sign up at **americangirl.com/email**
to receive the latest news and exclusive offers.